MR. MEN
Too Nosey

Roger Hargreaves

In these stories you will meet:

Mr Nosey

Mr Small

Mr Strong

Mr Tall

EGMONT
We bring stories to life

Book Band: Red

MR. MEN   **LITTLE MISS**

MR. MEN™ LITTLE MISS™ © THOIP (a SANRIO company)

Too Nosey © 2016 THOIP (a SANRIO company)
Printed and published under licence from Price Stern Sloan, Inc., Los Angeles.
Published in Great Britain by Egmont UK Limited
The Yellow Building, 1 Nicholas Road, London, W11 4AN

ISBN 978 1 4052 8265 9
63466/1
Printed in Singapore

Illustrated by Adam Hargreaves
Series and book banding consultant: Nikki Gamble

Written by Jane Riordan
Designed by Cassie Benjamin

MIX
Paper
FSC FSC® C018306

Too Nosey

This is Mr Nosey.

Hello, Mr Nosey.

Mr Nosey is nosey.

Mr Nosey is
too nosey.

Mr Nosey went out.

He had to look.

He did look.

He went in.
He had to look.

He went in. He went on.

He went up.

He went on and on.

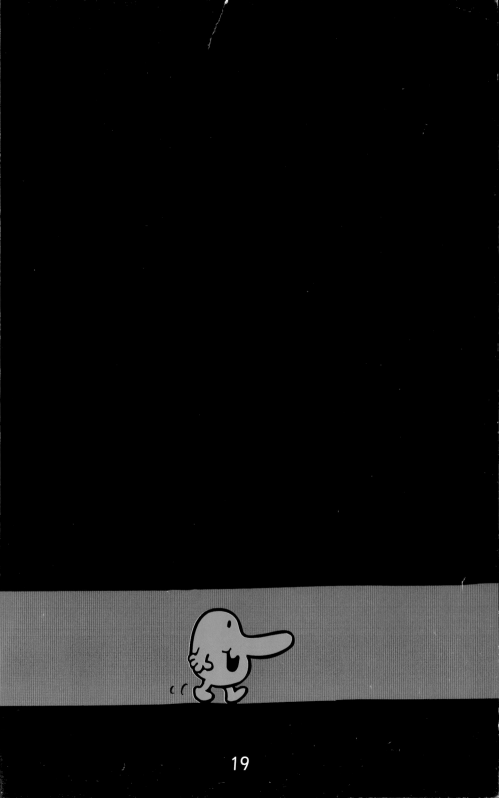

He had to look.

He went in.

Is that all?
I am too nosey!

Goodbye,
Mr Nosey!

This is Mr Small.

Hello, Mr Small.

Mr Small is small.

Mr Small is too small.

Mr Small got
bigger.

And bigger.

And *bigger!*

Look at Mr Strong!

Look at Mr Tall!

Goodbye, Mr Small or is it Mr Big?

On and On

Follow Mr Nosey in the maze. Go up and down to take Mr Nosey into the white room and then out again.

Start

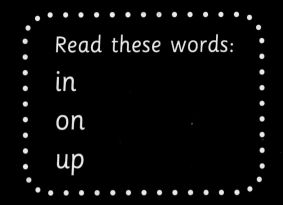

Read these words:

in

on

up

End

Big or Small?

Help Mr Small match the big objects to the word big and the small objects to the word small.

big

small